Emmy
the Exaggerating
Elephant

Fenton
the Fearful Frog

Gertie
the Grungy Goat

the Happy
Hamster

the Impatient
Iguana

Ollie
the Obedient
Ostrich

Perry
the Polite
Porcupine

Queenie
the Quiet Quail

Rupert
the Resourceful
Rhinoceros

Wendy
the Wise
Woodchuck

Xavier
the X-ploring
Xenops

Yori
the Yucky Yak

Ziggy
the Zippy Zebra

NOTE TO PARENTS

Perry's Not-So-Perfect Day
A story about good manners

Perry the Polite Porcupine always attempts to do and say the proper thing. His manners are impeccable, and he is always considerate of others. He tries his best to please his friends, but too often at his own expense. Then Perry finds out that you can say no and still be polite.

In addition to enjoying this story with your child, you can use it to teach a gentle lesson about the value of manners. Help your child understand that good manners make a good impression on others. Explain that when someone really doesn't want to do something, it's all right to say no, nicely but firmly.

You can also use this story to introduce the letter **P.** As you read about Perry the Polite Porcupine, ask your child to listen for all the words that start with **P,** and point to the objects that begin with **P.** When you've finished reading the story, your child will enjoy doing the activity at the end of the book.

The AlphaPets™ characters were conceived and created by Ruth Lerner Perle.
Characters interpreted and designed by Deborah Colvin Borgo.
Cover/book design and production by Norton & Company.
Logo design by Deborah Colvin Borgo and Nancy S. Norton.
Edited by Ruth L. Perle.
Grolier Books is a Division of Grolier Enterprises, Inc.   Printed and Manufactured in the United States of America

Perry's Not-So-Perfect Day

SARAH DAWSON

Illustrated by Deborah Colvin Borgo

GROLIER
B O O K S

One summer afternoon, Perry the Polite Porcupine stopped in the bookstore to say a friendly hello to Wendy the Wise Woodchuck.

"I see you have a new book about manners and etiquette," Perry said, picking the book up from the pile on the table. "This looks like the perfect book for me!"

"Seems to me you already know everything about good manners, Perry. You're always so polite and considerate of everyone," Wendy said.

"There's always something new to learn," Perry answered. "I'd like to buy it, please."

Perry paid for the book, and Wendy put it in a pretty paper bag.

Perry took the paper bag, thanked Wendy, and started for home.

Perry was just turning the corner, thinking about his new book, when Una the Unhappy Unicorn waved to him from her porch. As usual, Una looked upset.

"Perry! Perry!" she called.

Perry took off his cap and said, "Good afternoon, Una, is something wrong?"

"There's always something wrong," Una sighed. "I'm sure my pansies and petunias are getting too much sun today. Will you help me carry them up here?"

"Well, I'm on my way home to read my new book, but I'll be glad to help you," he said.

Perry carried all of Una's potted plants up the porch steps. Then he said good-bye to Una and continued on his way home.

Perry wanted to hurry, so he decided to take a short cut through the park.

On the way, he looked at his pocket watch. "When I get home, I'll fix myself a pot of tea and a peanut butter sandwich. Then I'll still have plenty of time to read my book," he said to himself.

Just ahead, some of the AlphaPets were having a big picnic. When they saw Perry, they called to him. Perry did not want to stop, but he knew it was not polite to ignore his friends, so he walked over to the picnic table.

"Hello, everybody!" he said, tipping his hat politely.

"Have you had dinner yet?" asked Rupert the Resourceful Rhinoceros.

"Well, er, ah, not really," answered Perry. "I'm anxious to get home and . . . and . . ."

"Perry, we are about to begin the most wonderfully delightful gourmet picnic!" exclaimed Emmy the Exaggerating Elephant. "We have pot roast, pickles, peas, parsley potatoes, popovers, pineapple, pears, and peaches. Plus . . . a giant pitcher of pink punch. And for dessert, I made a super duper pumpkin pie. Please join us. We all love your company."

"You *must* stay," Delilah the Demanding Duck insisted. "No ifs, ands, or buts."

"Well, then, I'll be glad to accept your kind invitation," said Perry. "It would be rude to refuse my friends," he said to himself.

Perry sat down at the picnic table. He put a napkin in his lap, and made sure that everyone was seated before he started to eat.

When Perry wanted something, he never grabbed. He politely asked someone to pass it. He waited until the platter of food was offered to him, and then he helped himself to a small portion. He used his fork and knife to cut his food, and he remembered to chew with his mouth closed.

When dinner was finished, Perry helped clear the dishes
and pack away the leftovers. Then he said, "The dinner
was delicious. Thank you very much for a very nice time."

Perry picked up his package and hurried home.

By the time Perry got home it was too late to read, so
he took a bath and put on his pajamas. He placed his
new book carefully on the night table. Then he turned
back his sheets, puffed up his pillows and got into bed.

As he was about to fall asleep, Perry thought,
"Tomorrow will be my very own, special, private, read-
all-day day! I can't wait!"

The next morning when Perry woke up, the sun was shining brightly.

"What a perfect day to sit by the pool and read!" he exclaimed.

So after Perry ate his pancakes, he took his book and settled himself in a comfortable chair near the pool.

Perry smiled to himself as he started to read his book.

Always say PLEASE *when you want something and* THANK YOU *when you get it.*

"Yes, I learned that a long time ago," Perry said. He read on.

Always say HELLO *when you arrive and* GOOD – BYE *when you leave.*

SHAKE HANDS *and* SMILE *when you meet someone.*

DON'T INTERRUPT *when someone is speaking.*

SAY EXCUSE ME *if you bump into someone or if you make a mistake.*

Perry knew all those manners already.

Perry was happily turning the pages of his book when he heard the doorbell ring.

"Perry! Perry! Is anybody home?" said a voice at the front door.

"I'm not expecting anyone," Perry said to himself. He put down his book and went to see what all the noise was about.

Perry opened the door. Tina the Truthful Tiger and Connie the Cuddly Cat were there.

"Hello, Perry," said Tina. "It's such a warm day, Connie and I thought we'd drop by for a swim in your pool. I hope you don't mind."

Perry knew it was polite to make his friends feel welcome but inside he was thinking, "Will I ever be able to read my book?" He smiled. "Well . . . er . . . Come right in," he said.

"Thank you!" whooped Tina and Connie. They followed Perry through the house to the backyard. Then they jumped in the pool with a *splash!*

Tina and Connie weren't the only ones who dropped by for a swim. Soon Bradley the Brave Bear arrived, and so did Monty the Mimicking Mouse and Albert the Absent-minded Alligator.

"Hi, Perry," said Bradley. "Perfect day, isn't it?"

"Hi, Perry," said Monty. "Perfect day, isn't it?"

"Yes, I guess it was ... er ... *is* a perfect day," Perry said, a little sadly. "It sure is hard being polite sometimes," he thought to himself.

Perry watched his friends having a wonderful time splashing in the pool. Then he had an idea! He took his book and quietly slipped into the house.

Perry ran to his bedroom, and found the perfect hiding place: his closet. He pushed his shoes aside, sat down on the floor, opened his book and continued to read.

ALWAYS BE PUNCTUAL. *Do not keep people waiting.*

Be respectful of others, but RESPECT YOURSELF, *too.*

"That's a *new* one. I wonder what it means," Perry said. He read on.

If you really don't want to do something, YOU CAN SAY "NO" POLITELY.

Perry's eyes lit up! "Oh, my goodness!" he said. "I never thought of it that way before! Being polite means treating people kindly—but it doesn't mean that I have to say yes *all* the time. I can say no in a kindly way, too!"

Perry ran out to the pool. "Listen, everybody!" he called. The AlphaPets stopped playing and listened to him.

"I want you all to have a good time, and I don't want to hurt your feelings, but . . . but . . ." Perry couldn't continue.

"What's wrong?" Connie asked.

"Please tell us!" said Tina.

"Well," Perry said. "You are all my friends and I love you, but I didn't expect you to drop in on me. I'm sorry, but I have other plans today."

"There! I said it," thought Perry. His heart was pounding.

The AlphaPets gathered around their friend.

"I hope you're not upset," Perry said softly.

"Not at all," said Bradley. "You were as polite as always. And it was brave of you to remind us to be considerate of you, too."

"Don't forget," said Albert, "friends should always tell each other how they really feel."

"Well, we'd better get going," said Tina. "Thank you for a very nice time, Perry. And next time, we'll remember to call first. Right?"

"Right!" everyone shouted.

"Right!" said Monty.

Will you please read these words with me?
Thank you.

purse

pencil

pineapple

pie

pajamas

puzzle

pillow

pickle

Look back in this book and try to find these
and other things that begin with P.

Know Your Alphabet

Aa Bb

Gg Hh

Mm Nn Oo Pp

Uu Vv Ww